Dress to Impress

Coleen
Style Queen

Dress to Impress

HarperCollins *Children's Books*

With thanks to Lucy Courtenay

First published in Great Britain by HarperCollins *Children's Books* in 2008.
HarperCollins *Children's Books* is a division of HarperCollins *Publishers* Ltd.
77-85 Fulham Palace Road, Hammersmith, London, W6 8JB.

1

Text copyright © Coleen McLoughlin 2008
Illustrations by Nellie Ryan/EyeCandy and
Nicola Taylor NB Illustration 2008

ISBN-13 978-0-00-727740-7
ISBN-10 0-00-727740-7

The author and illustrator assert the moral right to be
identified as the author and illustrator of the work.

Printed and bound in England by Clays Ltd, St Ives plc

One

So, I'm on the side of this freezing cold pitch, stamping my feet and totally wishing I had a special ankle heater. No disrespect to my little sister, but watching footie in the winter is a nightmare. Especially when there are no goals and the match is practically over.

Em plays on the wing in our local under-eights team. She's dead keen and brilliant with it, and the whole family goes to watch her most weekends. I'm proud and all, but why do footie matches always have to be so *cold*?

5

"Pass the ball, Em!" yelled my dad, racing past me with his whistle bouncing on his tracksuit like a twinkly silver necklace.

"I'm not sure your dad should be telling Em what to do, Coleen," Mum murmured to me as Dad pelted back the other way, still roaring instructions at my sister. "As the ref, isn't he supposed to be neutral?"

"Asking Dad to be neutral in a game of football would be like asking me to wear school uniform at the weekend," I announced between chattering teeth. I swear my toes were about to fall off.

Mum glanced at me from underneath her dark blue beanie hat. She had her famous annoyed-but-resigned look on her face. "Getting you to wear a *coat* would be a start," she said.

My outfit *was* a little summery for a cold day, I have to admit. But I'd spent ages customising my T-shirt that morning with a bunch of safety pins all threaded with these brilliant neon-coloured beads. They made excellent patterns all down the front and jangled when I walked. There was no way I was going to hide my handiwork underneath a coat.

"Boots might have been an idea too, Coleen," Mum said wearily. "Who on earth wears sandals in October?"

"I wanted to try out my new nail polish," I said, admiring my dark blue toenails. The cold was totally worth it every time I looked down.

"Your toes are practically as blue as the polish," said my best mate Mel.

Mel was more sensibly dressed than me, with a scarf wrapped tightly round her neck and a woolly hat with a peak at the front sitting neatly on her head. Beats me how she got it on over her crazy curls. The hat is new: we bought it together yesterday, and it totally rocks. The colours are perfect for her.

Standing beside Mel was my other mate Lucy. She's

gorgeous, with long blonde hair and blue eyes. Her plain blouses and ironed jeans drive me crazy, and I spend most weekends at the shops persuading her to try new stuff. She's as different from Mel as France and England – which makes me the Channel Tunnel, I guess, cos I'm the link that joins them together!

"Which one's Em again?" Lucy asked, peering across the windy pitch to where a blur of muddy knees and blue team strip identified the Hartley Juniors.

"Th... th... that one," I shivered, pointing to the far side of the pitch.

A small, brown-haired streak of mud and energy was flying down the wing, dribbling the ball like a pro. As we watched, a little blond lad raced up beside her. Em neatly passed him the ball, totally foxing the boy on the other team who'd been chasing her.

"Go, Em!" Mum yelled, clapping enthusiastically.

"Yay!" cheered Mel and Lucy.

Believe me, I wanted to clap. But my hands were tucked too tightly into my armpits. So I clapped like mad inside my head instead.

The blond lad who now had the ball for Hartley Juniors raced on down the pitch. He dodged a couple of opponents, and then lofted the ball right up and smack into the net, just as the final whistle went. Goal! Our side of the touchline erupted.

"Hart*lee*! Hart*lee*! One-nil!"

"Billy, Billy, Billy!"

"I guess that's Billy," Mum observed as Em and her team mates clustered around the blond lad and tried to lift him off the ground in celebration.

I squinted at the lad. I'd never seen him before. He was obviously a new member of the team. Then I forgot all about him as something blissfully warm settled down on my frozen toes.

"Rascal," I gasped, looking down at our hairy

black spaniel who had curled himself up on my feet. "You total hero!"

"Psst," Lucy whispered in my ear. "Coleen, look over there! He's *gorgeous*!"

I stared at where Lucy was pointing with one finger over her shoulder. A father and son were standing together on the touchline a little further along. Judging from how madly they were clapping and grinning and waving at the little blond goal-scorer as he trotted towards them, I guessed they were his family. The dad was tall and strong-looking, with close-cropped blond hair. The lad standing with him looked about the same age as us.

I have to say that I find most lads boring – with the massive exception of Lucy's older brother Ben. Ben Hanratty is *totally* the boy I'm going to marry one day, when he opens his eyes and sees that there's more to me than just his kid sister's mate.

But even I could see that the lad down the touchline was quite cute. He was blond, with a lovely straight nose and bright blue eyes whose colour you could see even in the sludgy October light.

"There's no need to be so *obvious*," Lucy hissed.

I whipped around and had this wild urge to giggle, which is a sure sign that I'm losing it. "Do you think he noticed us looking?" I mumbled.

Mel peeped over Lucy's head. "Yeah," she said with a grin, "I think he did. He's coming over."

Lucy groaned and hid her face in her hands. Sure enough, he was heading towards us. I bit down hard on my tongue, which made my eyes water but at least killed the giggles – for now.

"He's really looking at you," I said in a low voice to Lucy.

"As if!" Lucy squealed, sounding totally delighted.

The boy stopped beside Lucy. Lucy went bright

11

red and stared furiously at the ground. Unable to catch Lucy's eye, he turned to me instead. "That your sister then?" he said to me, nodding at Em as she jumped around with Dad up by the goal. "She made a really great pass."

"Thanks," I stuttered.

There was a funny silence. Lucy waggled her eyebrows madly at me, which I took to mean, "Keep him talking."

"Um…" I said. "That your brother then?"

I realised just too late that I sounded totally like a parrot. It was exactly the same question he'd just asked me, apart from the sister bit.

"Yeah," he nodded. "Billy's going to make us all famous one day." He grinned as he said it, then he glanced hopefully at Mel and Lucy. "All right?" he asked.

Mel grinned back. Lucy just looked like she wanted to sink into the ground and die right there.

 12

Lucy's funny like that – all shy around people she doesn't know, *especially* boys who obviously like her!

I quickly introduced myself and my mates.

"I'm Frankie Wilson," said the lad, "and the tall bloke's my dad. But don't try and talk to him," he warned. "He'll bore you to death with football statistics."

"He should meet my dad," I said. "There'd be a footie stat stand-off."

For some reason, I decided that this was the most hilarious thing I'd ever said. Snorting giggles roared out of me, huge and loud and uncontrollable. Frankie Wilson looked a bit surprised.

"Don't mind Coleen," said Mel as I howled away hopelessly. "It's a medical thing. Doctors from around the world can't cure her. There's nothing we can do except wait until they're over."

Frankie looked over at Lucy. "You always this quiet?" he asked with a gentle smile.

Lucy immediately blushed to the roots of her hair. What with me still in fits and Lu doing her beetroot thing, it was all down to Mel to keep Frankie talking.

"Lucy's a singer," Mel said. "She saves it for the stage."

Frankie raised his eyebrows. "Is that right?"

Lucy gave a tiny nod and stared at the sky.

"What stuff are you into?" Frankie pressed on, looking pleased to have started a conversation with Lucy at last.

"R'n'B," Lucy whispered.

Frankie grinned. "Cool," he said.

"Frankie!" yelled Frankie's dad, his arm wrapped around his younger son's muddy shoulders. "Time to go!"

Frankie scuffed the ground with the toes of his trainers. "Right," he said, sounding a bit reluctant. "Gotta go. See you around, yeah?" And giving Lucy one last shy smile, he hurried off.

 14

"Hey!" I said, starting forward. "What school do you—"

But the rest of my question was totally lost as I pitched right over and half-buried my nose in the mud. I'd forgotten about Rascal, who was still draped over my feet. And by the time I'd stood up again, and Mel and Lucy had stopped laughing their heads off, Frankie Wilson was out of sight.

"That was *so* embarrassing," I moaned. "First I stare like a crazy person, then I laugh like a snorting pig and then I fall over and get covered in mud! My top's ruined."

"It could be worse," Mel said.

"How?" I demanded.

Mel shrugged. "Dunno," she said honestly.

"Coleen?" Lucy said. "Could I… maybe… come to the footie again with you next week? It's been really fun."

"Sure you can, Lu," I said absently. Dad was

beckoning me. "Gotta go. See you in school tomorrow, yeah?"

With a wave to my mates, I headed across the pitch with my family in the direction of home.

"Look at the state of you!" said Mum as I caught up with her. "What happened?"

"Oh, nothing, Mum. Don't make a fuss."

"Well you'd better get cleaned up and change into something sensible when we get home."

"Yeah, yeah…"

"Billy Wilson's brother seems like a nice lad," Mum said.

"He's cool," I said. "I think he really likes Lucy."

"Billy's the best forward Hartley Juniors have ever had," Em said, slinging her footie boots over her shoulder and holding Dad's hand. "The Wilsons only just moved to Hartley last week. Wasn't his goal brilliant?"

"All set up by you, Princess," said Dad in the gruff voice he uses when he's getting emotional.

"Good on you, Em," I said, cuffing my little sister lightly round the head.

And then the whole world came crashing down around my ears.

There ahead of me was Ben Hanratty, walking towards us. And not only was he heading our way, but he had his arm draped over Jasmine Harris's shoulders.

I've never had anything against Jasmine Harris. She's another Year Ten like Ben, and she's tall and shiny-haired. But I *do* have a problem with her snuggling up to my crush.

"Isn't that Lucy's brother?" asked Mum as they came closer.

My eyes were glued to Ben. He was leaning towards Jasmine now. They were about to...

17

"See you later," I blurted to Mum and took off sideways, away from the path and the sight of Ben and Jasmine kissing. *Kissing.*

Ben Hanratty has a girlfriend!

Two

"What's up with you, Col?" Dad asked at dinner that night.

"Nothing," I muttered, prodding the green beans around my plate.

"The last time I saw a face that long, I was stood next to a crocodile," Dad continued.

"Ha, ha." I squinched up my face at Dad to show him that his joke was totally unfunny.

"Come on, love," Mum coaxed. "Eat up your tea. There's apple pie for afters."

19

My mouth watered a bit. Mum's apple pie is the best. She puts in loads of cinnamon and her pastry is always crumbly and sweet. But then I thought about Ben and Jasmine…

"Sorry, Mum," I said gloomily. "I'm not really hungry."

Em was still rabbiting on about Billy Wilson. "He's got the best right foot ever," she said between mouthfuls of chicken and beans. "And he tackles like a train. *And* he's starting at my school after half-term!"

"You'll be married before we know it," said Dad gravely, pouring himself a glass of water. "I'll book the church."

"Dad!" Em squealed, giggling at the thought of marrying Billy Wilson.

All this talk about marrying was putting me off my food again. What did Ben Hanratty see in Jasmine Harris? OK, so she was in Year Ten with Ben and I was

20

only a little kid in Year Eight, but that wasn't supposed to matter when it came to love. I decided gloomily that it was the height thing. I'm only a bit over five feet, while Jasmine is so tall she probably spends her free time pulling jumbo jets out of her hair. They say the best things come in small packages. It looked like Ben Hanratty thought differently.

"Apple pie," Mum announced, clearing the plates and putting a slice of pie each and a jug of thick, creamy custard down on the table.

With my mind still on Ben and Jasmine, it took me a while to register the pie. I should've moved quicker. Before I knew it, Em had scoffed her slice, snatched mine and was already gobbling it down.

"Emma!" Mum snapped. She only calls my sister Emma when she's done something naughty.

"Starving," Em mumbled between mouthfuls. "Col said she wasn't hungry."

I goggled at the empty pie dish. Maybe there were worse things than broken hearts after all.

Going back to school after half-term is always tough. You get into the holiday habit of late morning lie-ins, and then – *wham*! When I heard my alarm on Monday morning, I rolled over and turned it off, same as I'd done all week. Then I snuggled back down into my cosy duvet and drifted away again.

The next thing I knew, the covers had been whipped right off me.

"Coleen!" Mum said. "Don't you realise that it's eight fifteen? I've been calling you for the past twenty minutes. You're going to be late – get a move on!"

I shot out of bed like my PJs were on fire. My usual bus reaches the stop at around eight twenty-five every morning. Getting the bus after is always

22

pushing it as it usually gets caught up in the middle of Hartley's rush hour. Besides, it wouldn't have Mel and Lucy on it – and I *seriously* needed to talk to Lucy about Ben and Jasmine.

Mum left me to it as I swung around my bedroom like a boomerang. Knickers! An ironed shirt – some hope. Where was my school jumper? And my skirt?

"Mum!" I roared, hopping around as I wriggled into my tights. "Have you seen my—"

A jumper and skirt sailed through the door and landed at my feet.

"Cheers, Dad," I panted as my dad shook his head and jogged down the stairs.

"See you later, Coleen!" Em called, heading out the door with Mum.

I yanked my tie over my head, slid up the knot like a lasso and took the stairs in one leap. (This is only possible if you get the angle right and try not to put all your weight on the banister. I took the banister off the wall this one time, but that's another story.) Grabbing my school bag, an apple and a slice of bread, I sprinted through the front door and tore down the street like an Olympic athlete in uniform. Then I groaned. Despite my best efforts, I was too late.

Panting to a halt, I watched miserably as my bus honked past, gusting out a smelly whoosh of exhaust. Mel and Lucy were pressed to the glass, waving sympathetically at me, while Dave Sheekey – Ben Hanratty's best mate and the most annoying lad at Hartley High – pulled stupid faces at me out the window. Ten minutes to wait till the next bus, then twenty minutes of biting my nails as I got later and later for register. I slumped down on one of the bus-stop seats and pulled out my apple. It wasn't

24

all bad, I supposed. At least I could brush my hair. And I was sure I had some tic tacs somewhere...

At five to nine, I burst through the classroom door like one of those cowboys you see in films who gets hurled through a saloon window.

"Ta-da," I declared. "Not late!"

"Whoop-de-doo," drawled Summer Collins, my least favourite girl in the whole of my class. Summer's mates Hannah Davies and Shona Mackinnon sniggered on cue as Summer pushed back her long blonde hair with one hand. *Hello?* I thought. *Who is she trying to impress?*

"Sit down, Coleen," our form teacher Mr Andrews said. Mr Andrews is OK, if you dig goatees and physics. "We're almost at the end of register."

I hurried to my seat and flopped down beside my

mates. "Lucy," I began, keen to get to the bottom of the whole Ben/Jasmine thing as soon as possible.

"Ravi Singh?" Mr Andrews read from the register. "Daniel Thorburn?"

As Ravi and Daniel grunted at Mr Andrews, I realised Mel and Lucy were both looking weirdly at me.

"What?" I said, my hand going instantly to my head. Doing a high ponytail at a bus stop without a mirror never really works. Did it look totally awful? I'd never seen Lucy looking so pale and agitated. She didn't normally get freaked out by bad hair.

"Coleen," Mel whispered, "you know the footie at the weekend?"

"Like I'm going to forget what an idiot I made of myself," I said, lolling back in my chair. I couldn't work out why Mel was talking so quietly. No one ever whispered at register. "That Frankie lad we met was nice, wasn't he? I think he liked you, Lucy."

"*Shhhhh!*" Lucy hissed wildly.

"Tanya Williams?" Mr Andrews went on.

"Here, sir," said Tanya.

"And last of all, our new face," Mr Andrews said. "Frankie Wilson?"

At Frankie Wilson's name, I let out a loud snort. Again. Oh noooo. I swung around and gawped at the familiar-faced lad sitting at the back of the room. *Frankie Wilson?* Here at Hartley High?

"Present," said Frankie Wilson with a smirk. "And may I thank the lovely laydee two tables down for such a warm welcome."

I blushed like a tomato, while everyone in the room – especially Summer and her mates – laughed themselves sick. *Lovely laydee?* What a creep!

"Urrrrrgh," I growled at Mel and Lucy as Frankie Wilson capered around the back of the classroom, taking bows like some kind of clown while the whole room cheered. He had his blond hair gelled into spikes, and was wearing his school tie undone nearly to his belt. What was he playing at? I caught Summer's expression. She was totally drinking it in. Then I realised Summer's hair-tossing earlier had all been for Frankie's benefit. Tragic!

"What a loser," said Lucy as we all filed out of the classroom and headed for drama. "And he seemed so… nice at the footie."

"Lads always act like idiots in school, I guess," I said. It was pretty generous of me, given that my pride was still hurting.

"Especially when they're new," Mel agreed. "They've got to be all look-me-tough-guy, you know?"

I slung my arm around Lucy. "You OK?" I asked.

"I guess," Lucy mumbled. "It was just a shock, that's all."

"Talking of shocks," I said, keen to move on from

Frankie Wilson, "what's going on with Ben and Jasmine Harris?"

Mel gasped as I told them what I'd seen in the park after the footie. Lucy on the other hand didn't look very surprised.

"Jasmine was round ours most of half-term," she said. "It was really weird having her in the house. I was going to tell you at the footie, but then we met Frankie and... I kind of forgot."

"You really do like him, don't you?" I said.

"I *did*," Lucy said sadly. "But I don't any more. Who could fancy an idiot like that?"

"Summer Collins," I said. "Did you see all that hair-flicking back there?"

"*That's* what all that was about!" Mel said, acting all amazed. "There I was thinking maybe she was just swatting a bunch of flies around her head!"

Lucy gave a glimmer of a smile. Even though we

were doing our best to cheer her up, I could guess how she was feeling. Stupid, and annoyed, and disappointed. I thought about Ben and sighed. It looked like love just wasn't going our way.

Three

We were going round to Lucy's for tea after school. I'd had this whole outfit planned for Ben's benefit: my newly beaded T-shirt plus my favourite leggings and these cute little banana shoes that fold in half so you can carry them around in a teeny handbag. The whole ensemble folds down into practically nothing, and I'd been going to tuck them into my bag before school that morning. But you guessed it: in my bus panic, they got left behind.

"Don't worry about it, Coleen," said Lucy, unlocking

her front door as I stood and fretted with Mel out on the pavement. "Ben won't notice you anyway. He's bringing Jasmine back later on."

Like *that* was going to make me feel any better.

"No way!" I wailed.

"It must be really funny seeing Ben all loved up," Mel giggled.

Lucy made a face. "Gross, more like. His mates are really mad at him because he's not seen them all half-term. He's gone all Jasmine this, Jasmine that. I can't get a word of sense out of him."

"Can we change the subject?" I asked.

We went upstairs to Lucy's room, and Lu put on some really soulful music. It made me feel even worse. I was as jumpy as a kangaroo on a trampoline. My ears were on elastic for the front door. When we heard Ben's voice, I couldn't resist creeping out and peeping over the banister down into the hall. I so

wish I hadn't. Ben and Jasmine were giggling about something, their heads all close together.

"Stop torturing yourself, Col," said Mel over my shoulder. "Come back in with us. Lu wants some advice on what she should do about Frankie Wilson."

"I thought she didn't like Frankie any more," I said in surprise.

Mel rolled her eyes. "Who ever said lurve was logical?"

When you're suffering from a broken heart, talking about someone *else's* broken heart always helps. I followed Mel back into Lucy's room, where Lu was sitting on the edge of the bed looking all miserable.

"Weren't you going to forget about Frankie Wilson?" I said, plopping down beside her.

"I know," Lucy sighed. "But I can't. He was great at the footie, into the same music as me and everything. I've never met a boy I get on with so well.

It felt like we had a real connection. I think maybe he's just showing off in class so no one picks on him. Don't you think?"

She looked at me hopefully. I had a sudden memory of how Frankie had brought Lucy out of her shell at the footie. *That* was the real Frankie, I felt sure of it.

"We'll give him another chance tomorrow," I said at last. "Mention the football and see what he says."

"Tea's on the table!" Mrs Hanratty shouted from down in the kitchen.

I hunted around Lucy's dressing table until I found what I needed.

"Sunglasses?" Mel said in surprise as I slipped the sunnies on my nose.

"I just want something over my eyes so I don't have to look at Ben and Jasmine," I explained.

Mel and Lucy both burst out laughing.

34

"What are you like, Coleen?" Lucy said.

"Right now," I said, peering carefully around, "practically blind. These are the darkest sunnies in the world, Lu. Give us a hand down the stairs, will you?"

I'm pleased to say that the sunglasses worked – kind of. Squirting maple syrup on my chips instead of ketchup was a bit of a disaster, but it was a small price to pay.

"My brother thinks you are really weird, Coleen," Lucy informed me on the bus the next day.

I wasn't sure how I felt about this: pleased that Ben had noticed me, or worried that I'd looked downright daft? Glancing down the bus, I saw Ben and Jasmine sitting with their arms draped around each other in the usual Year Ten seats. Sitting opposite them, Ali Grover and Dave Sheekey, Ben's two mates, were looking well cheesed off. Ali was staring at the roof and Dave had his eyes firmly shut. It looked like I wasn't the only one who didn't approve of Ben's new girlfriend.

Lucy was all jittery as we walked down the school corridor to our form room. There was no sign of Frankie Wilson just yet. We settled down at our desks and waited.

"Have you noticed something?" Mel asked me. She nodded her chin in the direction of Summer Collins' table.

Summer had done her normally straight blond hair all in ringlets. They were pushed back off her face with a sparkly black hairband, and were falling down her back like a curly waterfall.

"She must've got up at six this morning to do that," I said. Even though I couldn't stand Summer, you had to admire her dedication.

"Ten out of ten for effort," Mel agreed.

 36

I glanced at Lucy, who was staring at her desk. Did she realise that Summer was totally after Frankie?

Mr Andrews came in with the register in his arms, balanced on top of a load of papers. He was about to set the teetering pile down on his desk when Frankie Wilson skidded into the classroom. His hair was gelled up more fiercely than ever. I watched Frankie stop, grin at Lucy – and then deliberately shove into Mr Andrews' back.

"Sorry sir," Frankie said cheerily as Mr Andrews' papers flew up into the air like enormous bits of confetti. "Didn't spot you there."

"Did you see that?" Mel gasped, starting to her feet.

I gawped down the classroom at Frankie. I couldn't believe what he'd just done. It seemed totally out of character. Plus now, the cheeky devil wasn't making any effort to help Mr Andrews pick everything up. Instead, he'd perched himself on the edge of

Summer's desk and was whispering something in her ear, making Summer and her mates all giggle. All my faith in 'the real' Frankie Wilson went *pop*. Mr Andrews was pretty boring, but what Frankie had done to him was plain nasty.

"There is no *way* we give him a second chance after that," I announced when the bell went.

"He smiled at me," Lucy said, looking confused. "Then he went and talked to Summer. What was that all about?"

"Boys," Mel said. "More trouble than they're worth."

Frankie suddenly loomed up in our path like some kind of monster from Scooby-Doo. "Whoo!" he shouted. "Cheer up, girls. It might never happen!"

"It just did," I said through gritted teeth as he zoomed off down the corridor. Summer, Hannah and Shona all followed, like hungry seagulls following a fishing boat. Pathetic!

38

We managed to avoid Frankie for the rest of the week. But avoiding his voice was a totally different matter. Everywhere we went, we could hear him gabbing on. He was full of his little brother Billy's footballing talents, what a big house they had, how his dad had just bought a new car… blah, blah, blah – he just went on and on. It was amazing how much he had to say, and how loudly he said it. By the end of the week, the whole of Year Eight was in love with Frankie Wilson, it seemed – apart from us. As far as we were concerned, it was a relief to reach the weekend and escape.

"I don't think I'll come to the footie this week," Lucy said apologetically as we headed to the bus stop on Friday after school. "Do you mind, Coleen?"

"Course not," I said. "The match is over the other side of Hartley on Sunday, anyway."

"Are you still going?" Mel asked me.

I nodded. "We always go to Em's matches. But if Frankie Wilson's there, I swear I'll turn my back and ignore him."

"That might be easier said than done," Mel said as Frankie Wilson raced past blowing a very loud, very wet raspberry.

"Try me," I said in a voice that would curdle custard.

Another cold Sunday, another football match. I'd listened to Mum this time, and was wearing my old puffa jacket and a pair of trainers. The only thing I had done was take off the buttons and sew them back on with silver thread. You've got to have a *bit* of bling on a freezing cold touchline, right?

"There's that Wilson lad," said Mum, nodding down the touchline to where I could see Frankie and his dad huddled together with Billy.

"I noticed," I muttered.

Mum looked surprised at my tone of voice. "What's up with you?" she asked. "I thought you and your friends liked him."

"A lot can happen in a week," I said, stamping my feet on the muddy grass.

Dad wasn't refereeing today, but it hadn't stopped him getting into his tracksuit. I could see the outline of his whistle tucked into his top pocket as he jogged up and down the touchline, watching Em like a hawk as she moved around the pitch.

"Hiya."

I nearly jumped out of my skin. Frankie Wilson had sneaked up without me noticing and was now standing next to me.

"Hi," I grunted, determined not to talk to him any more than I could help.

"No mates today?" he asked, glancing down the touchline.

I couldn't help the sarcasm from creeping into my voice. "Funnily enough, no."

Frankie didn't seem to notice. If anything, he looked disappointed. After a minute, he felt around in his coat pocket. "I brought this for Lucy," he said, holding out a CD to me. "It's my favourite CD from my dad's collection. I thought maybe she'd like to download it and…"

I must've had a face like a bulldog chewing a wasp because he tailed off when he clocked my expression. "Sorry," he mumbled, tucking the CD back into his pocket. "Whatever. Tell her I said hi, yeah?" And he turned around abruptly and headed back up the touchline to his dad.

42

Weird, I thought to myself. Why all Mister Too Cool For School one day, and nice as anything the next?

To be honest, I felt the teeniest bit guilty. He'd brought that CD especially for Lucy, after all. I could kind of understand the clowning around in class – I mean, if it was friends that Frankie Wilson wanted, he'd made more in a week than me in my whole first term at Hartley High. But if he liked Lucy, why was he playing up to Summer at school? I didn't understand it, but then I can't say I understand lads much.

Hartley Juniors lost their match, so there was no reason to hang around chatting. I got Dad to drop me in town on the way home. Mel and Lucy were waiting for me at our usual weekend meeting place in the market square.

"Unbelievable," I said, shaking my head.

"What?" Mel said, all agog. "Was Frankie there?"

"Yes," I said. "All nice as pie again. And get this. He even brought a CD for Lucy!"

"He did *what*?" Lucy repeated.

"You heard," I grinned. It was hard not to smile when you saw the look on Lucy's face.

"What CD was it?" Lucy asked eagerly.

I waggled my eyebrows at her. "'My favourite CD from my dad's collection'," I quoted, putting two fingers down my throat and gagging.

"And he brought it for *me*?" Lucy gasped. "So have you got it?"

"Sorry, Lucy," I said. "I kind of – gave him a few evils. He took it back."

Lucy started to say something when Mel held up her hands. "No, no, no!" she warned. "We are not going down the 'Frankie Wilson is misunderstood' route again, you hear? You did the right thing, Coleen."

Lucy was blushing. "Maybe I will come to next

week's footie after all," she said. "If Frankie's too shy to talk to me at school, we'll just save it for the touchline."

"Shy?" I gasped, thinking of him clowning around in class. "I don't think shy is the right word, somehow. But there's definitely something odd going on. Still," I shrugged, "if you want to come to football, Lucy, that's fine by me."

By Monday morning, I was feeling totally confused about Frankie. Everything was as clear as mud to me as we climbed off the bus and headed in to school.

"Maybe Frankie's brought the CD to school," Lucy said hopefully as we reached our classroom door.

"Some hope," Mel snorted. She didn't buy the whole Frankie being a nice guy thing either, even though Lucy had spent the entire bus trip trying to persuade us.

We pushed through our classroom doors. Frankie was already in his seat. I was all prepared to smile forgivingly at him for Lucy's sake when I clocked who he was sitting with – and whose hand he was holding.

"Hi Coleen," Summer Collins simpered. "Nice weekend?"

Four

"**M**aybe there's a totally simple explanation," I said hopefully the following Saturday.

"There is," Mel said at once. "Frankie Wilson's a two-timing twerp."

"We've had this argument about a million times," Lucy said wearily. "Frankie's going out with Summer, end of story. You saw them together this week, Coleen. Holding hands in the playground and everything."

"But he still smiled at you in the dinner queue yesterday, Lucy," I pointed out, feeling confused.

"Exactly," Mel said with a fierce nod. "A two-timing turnip."

Me and Lucy both had to giggle at that one.

We were round at Lucy's again, trying to decide whether we were going to the footie this weekend or not. Even though Em's my little sister and everything, there are times when you have to stand by your mates.

"If you don't want to go today, I won't go either," I declared.

"But Coleen, what about your sister?" Lucy wailed.

"Em'll be so busy scoring goals she won't even notice," I fibbed.

Between you and me, my little sister takes the whole family-on-the-touchline thing pretty seriously. Something to do with luck – and the chocolate bars Mum always has in her handbag at the end of a match. But the chocs would still be there with or without me, and mates are mates, right?

"If we want to support Em, then Frankie Wilson's got no right stopping us," Mel announced, folding her arms.

"When did you become such a fan of Hartley Juniors, Mel?" I asked in surprise. "You only came the once."

"It's the *principle*," Mel said stoutly.

Don't get Mel started on principles. She'll stick to them till she's blue in the face, and you along with her.

"I think we should go," Lucy said.

I was gobsmacked. "Really? But what if Frankie's there with Summer?"

"No problem," Lucy said firmly. "Just because Frankie's got a girlfriend, doesn't mean we can't be mates, does it?"

"Good on you, girl," said Mel, clapping Lucy on the back and making her cough.

"We *so* need perfect outfits for this," I declared, now the decision was made. "The kind of look that says 'don't mess with me', but doesn't try too hard, you know?"

"Whatever you say, Coleen," Lucy said, shaking her head at me.

I bent over my bag and rummaged through handfuls of scarves, belts and jewellery. I had been hoping that Lucy would come around to the idea of the footie, as I hate disappointing my kid sister. So I'd put together an emergency supply of accessories to make any outfit look cool, even Lucy's safer-than-safe jeans and T-shirts.

"Plenty to choose from here," I said, tipping out the lot.

Everything made a lovely clattering noise as it fell among the teddies and lacy cushions that decorate Lucy's bed.

"Great earrings," Mel said, pouncing on a pair of turquoise wooden hoops and holding them up to her ears.

I squinted at Mel's outfit. She was wearing brown

jeans today, with a funky belt and a skinny-rib white polo neck.

"Try that," I said, pointing at a heavy wooden necklace that I'd found in my nan's jewellery box when I was nine. I'd liked it so much that Nan had given it to me.

"Cool," Mel murmured, taking the wooden necklace and slipping it round her neck. It hung all chunky and fabulous, just like I'd pictured it.

Lucy was staring doubtfully at this cute little beanie hat I'd brought along especially for her. "It's a bit..." she began.

"Stop fussing and put it on," I pleaded. "It'll look brilliant, Lucy. Honest."

Lucy pulled the beanie over her long blonde hair. "I feel like a scarecrow," she said, peering out from underneath it.

"You look great," I declared, smoothing her hair

down over her shoulders. "Funky and I-don't-care."

"If you say so," Lucy sighed.

"Two thirty, guys," Mel said suddenly. "Doesn't the match start at three?"

We piled the accessories into my bag and raced down the stairs. When I caught sight of Ben and Jasmine in the kitchen, I automatically covered my eyes, crashed into Mel's back and landed in a heap on Lucy's doormat.

"They weren't even kissing," Lucy pointed out as she and Mel hauled me back to my feet.

"Sorry," I said sheepishly. "Automatic."

We reached the touchline just as the whistle went. The first person I saw on the pitch was Billy Wilson, hurtling past us. The wind was behind him, and it made him extra fast. Standing in their usual spot were Frankie

and his dad. Frankie glanced in our direction at once.

"Summer's not here," I whispered to Lucy.

Lucy smiled with relief. The wind was making her look extra pretty, with her rosy cheeks and sparkly eyes. Sadly, you couldn't say the same about me. If I crossed my eyes, I could see that the tip of my nose was bright red.

"Look out," Mel muttered. "The turnip is approaching."

Lucy's hand flew to her hat.

"Leave it!" I hissed, stopping her from pulling it off. "Do you want your hair blowing in your eyes?"

Frankie glanced nervously at me as we all shuffled around to face him. Pulling up my scarf a little, I tried not to look at him.

"So," Lucy began with a squeak in her voice. "Coleen says you brought me a CD last week."

"I brought it again, just in case you came today,"

Frankie said, fumbling around in his pockets.

"Very nice of you, I'm sure," said Mel in a sarcastic voice.

"Look, Mel," I said loudly, taking Mel's hand and pulling her away from Lucy and Frankie. "Em's doing a brilliant tackle."

"What are you doing, Coleen?" Mel asked crossly. "I wanted to keep an eye on Lucy."

"I think maybe Lucy's got to work this out by herself," I said. "Anyway, she's fine. Look at her."

We both looked. Lucy and Frankie were chatting like they'd known each other for ages. I got a warm feeling in my tummy that things were going to work out just fine, even after everything that had happened at school.

Then a roar on the pitch caught our attention.

"GOOOAAALLL!"

"It's Em!" I squealed, pointing at the jumping Hartley

Juniors around the away goal. "I think she just scored!"

As usual, Dad had forgotten he was supposed to be a neutral referee. He had thrown himself into the muddle of celebrating players and lofted Em up on to his shoulders, where she waved at me, Mum and Mel with a grin that practically wrapped round her whole head.

Frankie and Lucy had appeared beside us again. Lucy looked like she was floating a couple of centimetres off the ground.

"Top goal from your sister, Coleen," Frankie said.

"She's all right, our Em," I said gruffly, like I wasn't the proudest sister in the whole world right then.

Frankie checked his watch. "I have to go now," he said, sounding really sorry about it. "I promised Mum I'd pick up a bit of shopping for her. Hope the rest of the match goes OK."

He grinned sheepishly at Lucy, then stuck his hands in his pockets and headed out of the park.

"Spill," I ordered as soon as Frankie Wilson was out of earshot.

Lucy giggled and linked arms with us both. "He was really lovely," she said. "All friendly, not like he is at school at all."

"Did he explain about Summer?" Mel asked.

"I didn't mention her, and neither did he," Lucy said with a shrug. "We didn't talk about school at all, actually. Just music. And our date next weekend."

"A DATE?" me and Mel both screeched at once.

"Well, kind of a date," Lucy said happily. "We're meeting at The Music Place."

The Music Place had just opened in Lions' Walk, the local shopping mall. It had always been a music store, but it had just had a total makeover. Apparently, there were these listening booths now where you could check out new tunes, and banks of computers to do downloads straight to your MP3 player, and a little café with old records hung around the walls. I couldn't wait to see it for myself.

"You *agreed* to a *date* with *Frankie Wilson*?" Mel said, sounding shocked.

I knew where Mel was coming from. I was really pleased that Lucy and Frankie had got on so well, but...

"But why didn't you ask him about Summer?" I asked.

"It was too embarrassing," Lucy confessed. "But as I said, he didn't mention her," she added hopefully, "so maybe she's not his girlfriend any more?"

I didn't know what to say. There was something here that I didn't understand. It was like chasing fog down the playground, only to find that the fog had somehow moved up the end you just came from.

I opened my mouth, wondering what was going to come out. But whatever it was got lost in the massive yell of disappointment sweeping down our side of the touchline. The away side had just scored.

Sunday dinner is an event round our house, as Nan always comes to join us. She lives a few streets down in the house where Dad and his brothers were all born. My Pops died when I was five. I find it hard to remember him, and Em can't remember him at all. But once you meet my nan, you never forget her. She's still dead glamorous at fifty-nine, her fingernails always painted and her tiny feet tucked into the most brilliant high-heeled shoes. My first memory is of teetering around in a pair of them. To tell the truth, trying on Nan's shoes is still my favourite thing to do when we go round to hers. She's definitely where I get my interest in fashion. It's in my genes.

Anyway, you can always rely on Nan to tell a bunch of embarrassing stories about Dad when he was a toddler or a teenager at our Sunday dinners. Me and Em always make sure to get her on the subject as soon as we can.

"Tell us about the time you did that chocolate cake for Dad's birthday," I pleaded as Mum poured us all cups of tea after dessert.

Dad groaned and banged his head on the table. "Not that one," he said into the tablecloth.

"Don't be so daft, Kieran love," said Nan comfortably. "You weren't the first nine-year-old to eat so much chocolate cake on his birthday that he was sick. Being sick into the fireplace, though – that was a little more unusual."

Em snorted into her cup and sent a jet of brown tea shooting across the table. Well, that just set me off. I sat there and hooted like a crazy owl.

"You're one to laugh, Coleen," Mum said. "Need I remind you of how loudly you sang 'Mary, Mary, quiet and hairy' in your primary-school concert? There we all were, picturing poor old Mary with a full moustache."

"No one explained it was supposed to be *contrary*!" I spluttered indignantly as Em screamed with laughter. "I still don't even know what contrary means!"

"Mary, Mary, Col's getting lairy," Em sang, ignoring my efforts to kick her under the table.

"On the subject of music," Dad said, "did you hear how they've revamped Vinny's Vinyl in the shopping mall, Mum?"

"They never!" Nan gasped. "The old record store?"

"Yes, it's called The Music Place now," I said, talking extra loudly to drown out Em's next *Mary, Mary* verse. "There's meant to be all these booths for listening to new tracks, and computers where you can download music."

Nan went totally misty-eyed. "Just like in my day,"

she sighed, setting down her tea. I swear I saw a tear glimmering in the corner of her eye.

"They didn't have computers in your day, Nan," I said kindly, thinking she was getting muddled.

"MP1 players back then, weren't they, Mum?" Dad joked.

"Not computers, you daft beggar," Nan said, waving one hand at Dad to get him to shut up. "Vinyl records! I met Kieran's dad over a Beatles track in one of the old booths in that store," she told the rest of us. "How about that? *All You Need Is Love.* How right they were."

"Did you know this, Kieran?" Mum asked my dad.

"Of course I did," Dad said. "That track got played to death in our house."

I got this huge, warm, snuggly feeling right in the pit of my stomach as I pictured Nan and Pops' eyes meeting over an old record. I tried to imagine it with me and Ben.

"That's dead romantic, Nan," I sighed.

Nan was smiling, lost in some old memory of Pops. "Your grandad was a real Jack the Lad back then," she said. "All bluster, mind. Underneath that quiffed hair and those old leather jackets he was as soft as butter."

Pops sounds a bit like Frankie Wilson, I thought. Maybe it was a sign that Lucy's date with Frankie at The Music Place was going to be OK after all. Maybe *they* would get married, and end up having dinner with their grandkids one day. How was that for a crazy thought?!

Five

"Look," I hissed to my mates as we cleared our dinner things at school the next day. "At least Frankie's done *something* right."

Summer was sitting at a table down the dining hall with a face like a bad-tempered wasp. Hannah and Shona were both trying to put their arms round her, but she kept shoving them away. At a different table, Frankie was kidding around with Ravi Singh and totally ignoring Summer. It looked like that little romance was well and truly over.

"If he's dumped Summer, he must like Lucy for real, don't you think?" I said happily. I was still feeling very warm and cosy about my grandparents, and was quite happy to give Frankie Wilson the benefit of the doubt today.

"He still hasn't spoken to Lucy today, though, has he?" Mel pointed out. "That's *well* suspect in my book."

"I don't care," said Lucy, going pink like she always did when we talked about Frankie.

"Course you do," I said. "No one likes being ignored."

Frankie was now taking a run and leapfrogging over Ravi. Both boys yelled and raced for the dining-hall doors. They reminded me of puppies that needed a walk.

"Let's follow them," I suggested. "See if we can get Frankie on his own outside."

Our school playground is massive. There's climbing equipment in one corner, and basketball markings on

the tarmac around a couple of scruffy nets. Kids were swarming around it in a wash of blue and grey uniforms. We stood and watched as Frankie and Ravi whipped around the basketball posts with a bunch of other Year Eight lads, trying to jump up high enough to touch the nets. When Ravi left the court to grab a drink out of his bag, we seized our chance.

"All right, Frankie?" Mel said.

Frankie was out of breath from running at the basketball nets. "Hot," he said, and did his eyebrow-waggling thing at us like he does when he thinks he's said something clever.

"I really love the CD," said Lucy nervously. "Thanks."

"Whatever," said Frankie, gazing over our shoulders as Ravi headed back towards him.

"So," Lucy struggled on, "are you still on for this weekend?"

Frankie leaped into the air and high-fived Ravi.

"What's happening this weekend?" he asked on the way back down again.

Mel and I exchanged glances. It was time to get Lucy out of what was turning into one of those awful embarrassing situations that you have nightmares about for weeks afterwards.

"You know," Lucy said a little desperately. "The Music Place? We said twelve on Saturday, right?"

At last we had Frankie Wilson's full attention. After a minute, he smiled.

"Noon on Saturday it is, dollface," he said, cocking his finger like a pistol and pretending to shoot us. "I hear The Music Place is cool."

"Great," Lucy said, looking puzzled, but massively relieved. "Well. See you."

"Wouldn't wanna be ya," Frankie sang at us, before leaping off after Ravi and the basketball hoops again.

"See?" Lucy said happily as we went back inside. "Told you everything would be OK."

"Well, not quite OK," Mel whispered in my ear as we joined the throng pushing through the doors at the bell. "He's back to his awful self. I don't like this."

"Me neither," I murmured. Inside I was thinking: *Dollface?* All those warm and cosy thoughts about Frankie and Lucy being like Nan and Pops were fizzling out like an old firework.

"What are we going to do?" Mel whispered.

"Frankie Wilson is *definitely* up to something," I said under my breath. "We have to be with Lucy on that date, Mel. Then it's up to us to work out what's going on, before Lucy gets hurt!"

Lucy was on a total high for the rest of the week. She didn't seem to notice the way Frankie whispered with Ravi every time we went past, or the way he said "Hiya, dollface" in this smarmy way at registration each morning. Summer glared at Lucy like she was a bit of gum on the bottom of her shoe, but Lucy didn't notice that either.

The only slight problem with this mood was that Lucy's confidence was up in the clouds too.

"You don't need to come to The Music Place with me," she insisted when I suggested that me and Mel joined her and Frankie at the weekend. "Honestly."

"But Lu—" Mel began.

"Mel," Lucy said firmly, "it would feel too weird having my mates along. It's much easier to talk to Frankie when I'm on my own. I'll be fine; I promise."

And nothing me and Mel said could make Lucy change her mind. We had to think of some other way of being on that date – and fast.

"It's an amazing thing, love," I said to Mel as we all waited for the bus home on Friday night. "Its like armour."

"What are you on about, Coleen?" said Mel.

"The way Lucy is now," I explained, "she could walk through a minefield and not notice the bombs as they popped around her. Look at her."

I grabbed Lucy's shoulder and swung her round. "Boo!" I shouted in her face.

"Coleen," Lucy laughed gently, pushing me away, "don't be so daft."

"See?" I said, turning back to Mel. "Whenever I do that to Em, it scares the socks off her. But loved-up Lucy? Cool as a cucumber in sunglasses."

"On an ice floe," Mel grinned, looking convinced by one of my theories for once. "In Alaska maybe, during the winter – drinking a Slushie."

As we giggled, our bus rumbled down the hill towards us. We gathered our stuff and climbed aboard, but Lucy stayed where she was, staring down the road and humming something that was probably off Frankie's dad's CD.

"Earth to Lucy," Mel called, speaking really slowly and clearly. "This is a bus. You get on. When you reach your stop, you get off. *Comprende?*"

"You're such a laugh, Mel," Lucy said dreamily, floating up the bus steps behind me.

"Hurry up, Jas!" came a familiar voice further down the road.

"Wait up, Ben. I've got a stitch, OK?"

Boing, boing, boing went my stomach, up and down like an elevator on elastic. Ben Hanratty was nearly at the stop, his bag flying over his shoulder. With a face like thunder, Jasmine Harris was running after him, wailing: "Wait, will you? Just *wait!*"

"You coming?" the bus driver asked as Ben

70

hesitated outside the doors. "Only this bus has to be somewhere else in a couple of minutes."

Ben looked like he couldn't make up his mind, one foot on the bus and one on the pavement. Jasmine was still running, yelling: "Wait!"

"Get on, Hanratty, you big girl's blouse," Dave Sheekey shouted from his usual place midway down the bus.

Ben jumped aboard and the doors hissed shut. Dave and Ali Grover both cheered at the sight of Jasmine Harris dumping her bag on the pavement and shaking her fist at the window as Ben sheepishly sat down.

"Good one, mate," said Dave, punching Ben on the shoulder.

"Jas'll give you an earful tomorrow," said Ali happily.

My heart expanded like a balloon. If Jasmine Harris's expression was anything to go by, it wouldn't be long before Ben Hanratty got dumped.

I was in a great mood when I woke up on Saturday. Happily imagining Jasmine and Ben breaking up, I bounced out of bed like Tigger at nine o'clock sharp. Me and Mel were meeting Lucy in town that morning, and we were going to find her the perfect date outfit.

Top tip: when shopping, dress as comfortably as you can. If you're going to be in and out of changing rooms, you don't want belts and buckles and tights – and you want to avoid all-in-ones *big* time. I pulled on my skinny black jeans, a pale pink tee and my silvery bomber jacket. Slipping my feet into pumps – laces are another big shopping no-no – I got my rucksack and headed out after a couple of pieces of toast and a wave at Mum.

"Try and find something special for your Nan's birthday when you're out, will you, Coleen?" Mum

72

called after me. "Turning sixty is a big thing for her."

Nan's birthday is two weeks tomorrow. Dad wanted to do a big party that weekend, but our house just isn't big enough. So we are going to do a special birthday tea on the Saturday for just the family with presents round at ours instead.

Thinking about Nan's present got me right into the town centre in what felt like a blink of time. Chocolates? Soap? What do grandmothers like? Shoes are all very well, but totally out of my price range.

"I've already seen what I want to get," Lucy said in excitement as soon as we'd all met up in our usual spot in the market square at ten.

"For my *nan*?" I asked dopily. My head was still swirling with soap and chocs.

"No, silly, for my date with Frankie," Lucy said, looking at me weirdly. "I just need you and Mel to tell me if it's OK."

"You must have got into town dead early if you've already been window-shopping," said Mel.

"I saw it last night," Lucy explained. "Mum and Dad, me and Ben went out for dinner at Luigi's, and it was there in the shop window next door, staring at me."

"Special occasion, was it?" I asked, hoping Lucy might say something like: "Ben needed cheering up because Jasmine dumped him on the phone last night."

"Mum's fortieth birthday," Lucy told us.

My birthday radar went *beep-beep-beep*. "What did you get her?" I asked eagerly. "I'm looking for something really special for my nan's sixtieth."

"Tea towels," Lucy said.

"Tea towels?" Mel repeated. "Man, I hope I don't get given tea towels when I'm forty."

"They were special ones," Lucy protested as I burst out laughing. "She did ask for them – honest!"

We were walking down Foxton Row, the best

street in Hartley for gorgeous fashion. I stared around at the windows with a sigh of pleasure. There was so much to look at. Millions of ideas swooshed around in my head as I looked at what was on display.

"We're not going in here!" Mel spluttered as Lucy stopped outside Forever Summer – the chicest and most expensive boutique on the street – that just happens to belong to Summer Collins' dad.

"Course not," said Lucy, sounding shocked. "I just need to fix my shoelace!"

Our budget was a lot less than the cheapest thing in Forever Summer. Lucy hurried us on around the corner. Standing beside Luigi's Pizzeria was a little charity shop that often had quirky things on its rails.

"There," Lucy said breathlessly.

"Good choice, Lu!" I said, staring at the little jacket that hung on the window dummy.

"And only four ninety-nine," said Mel, staring at

the label approvingly. "That's my kind of bargain."

Charity shops rock. You always find unusual stuff that no one else has got, they're cheap and you're doing your bit for charity. Win-win, as my dad would say.

We went in and Lucy tried on the jacket. It looked even better on her than I had hoped. It was a pale blue linen, with short flared sleeves and a wide tie-belt. It looked like it dated back to the sixties, but was *so* totally now.

"Put it over a long-sleeved white tee and jeans," I suggested, as Lucy twirled around the shop. "You'll look super-cool, but not overdressed. *Perfecto!*"

"Overdressed would be better than not dressed at all," Mel said suddenly, her eyes widening as she caught sight of the clock over the till. "It's eleven o'clock already, guys. We've only got an hour to get back to Lucy's, get Lucy changed and get her to The Music Place!"

As Lucy squealed and paid for the jacket extra fast, Mel glanced at me and raised her eyebrows. I patted the large rucksack I was carrying and winked.

When Lucy had refused to let us join her on her date with Frankie, me and Mel had come up with a different plan. Secrecy was essential if it was going to work. But if it *did* work, whatever Frankie Wilson was planning wouldn't get past *us*. Me and Mel were on Mate On Date Alert.

Six

"I… think… I'm… going… to… die…" I wheezed, collapsing against the wall outside Lions' Walk forty-five minutes later. "I've got a stitch and my T-shirt's all gross and sweaty!"

Lucy looked at the rucksack I had dumped on the pavement. "No wonder you're out of breath," she said. "That thing looks like it weighs a ton. What's in there, Coleen?"

"Just stuff," I said quickly. I really didn't want Lucy looking at my rucksack too closely. It

held the key to me and Mel's big plan.

"The main thing is that we made it," Mel said before Lucy could ask any more tricky questions. "You look fantastic, Lu, and we're even fifteen minutes *early*. How about that?"

It was true. Lucy looked totally brilliant, even after pegging it from the bus stop in record time. We'd done her hair in these two cute bunches, and her eyes were all sparkly from running. I would like to think that I looked sparkly-eyed too, but one glance in the nearest shop window told me that I was bright red in the face.

"I'm getting really nervous now," Lucy giggled, tweaking her bunches. "Will you come in with me – until Frankie gets here?"

"Sure, Lu. But don't worry, you'll be fine," I panted. "Trust us."

"We'll make sure of it," Mel whispered to me as

we walked into the shopping arcade together. "Right, Coleen?"

"Right."

Lions' Walk was built in the sixties. It's not the prettiest place you ever saw, but someone recently had the bright idea of painting the shops all different colours. Now it feels like stepping inside a crazy rainbow. It has some brilliant shops that are all way cheaper than Foxton Row, and what's not to like about that?

Today, the whole place had that fab Saturday buzz. People were strolling about carrying bags, chatting to mates, laughing and talking on their phones.

The Music Place was about halfway down the mall. Back when it had been plain Vinny's Vinyl, the shop front had been painted black. I guess it had been cool once, but it had got dead tatty. Now it was a rocking red, with a huge cream and black coloured sign with *The Music Place* written in this funky

sixties lettering hanging over the big glass doors.

Inside there were two different levels. The lower bit had these cream-coloured listening booths with swing doors like changing rooms all lined up along the back wall, which was painted a maroon colour. Computer stations stood at the far end, and the rest of the floor was filled with racks of CDs and DVDs. Then you went up these steps to the café, which stood on its own level behind shiny chrome railings. The tables and chairs were all bright red, the floor was black and white, and this gorgeous multicoloured old Wurlitzer jukebox stood in pride of place beside the counter.

"Wow!" Mel gasped as we gawped around like tourists. "This place looks so *different*!"

"It's brilliant," I said happily.

Lucy dashed to the CD racks while Mel went to check out the computers. I walked to the back of the store and peeped inside one of the listening booths.

Two sets of headphones hung beside two tall swively stools covered in shiny white material. A CD player was built into the wall.

"Try before you buy," said a voice behind me. "Choose a CD in the store and come and listen to it with a friend. It's the way we always used to do it."

I turned round to see a plump old man with white hair that stuck up like a dandelion clock, smiling at me over the swing doors.

"It's a great idea," I said.

"The old ideas are always the best ideas," said the man. "When I first opened this place, we had booths. Then they went out of fashion. I'm so glad my son has decided to bring back a touch of the old days."

"Are you Vinny?" I asked cautiously. "As in, Vinny's Vinyl?"

"Vincent O'Hara, at your service," said the old man. "My son runs this place now I've retired."

82

"My nan used to come here in the sixties," I said, stroking one of the white plastic stools.

"Maybe she sat on that very stool," Mr O'Hara laughed. "We brought them out of retirement for the store's new look. They've been in my garage for over thirty years, and they look as good as new, don't they?"

"They're really cool," I agreed.

Fashion could be very weird sometimes, I decided as Mr O'Hara gave me a little wave and disappeared. It was hard to believe that these gorgeous stools had once been so uncool that they'd been stuck in a garage. I was really glad they were back again.

Mel's head appeared over the swing doors of the booth. "Five to twelve, Coleen," she said urgently. "Lucy's getting restless."

Lucy had found a place at one of the café tables. A pile of about ten sugar lumps stood in a little tower on the table in front of her.

"What if he doesn't come?" she gabbled, adding another sugar lump to her tower. "What if he's forgotten? What if—"

"Chill, Lucy," I said. "Everything's going to be fine."

"We'll just – er – pop around the shops for a bit," said Mel, shooting me a glance. "We'll come back later. OK?"

"OK, thanks," Lucy whispered, fiddling frantically with the sugar lumps. "Oh…"

"She's losing it," Mel whispered to me as we both bent down to pick up the scattered sugar lumps off the floor. It was two minutes to twelve.

"See you then, Lu!" I said, giving my green-faced mate a cheerful wave. "Have a great time! I'm sure Frankie'll be here any minute!"

Me and Mel made a big thing of heading for the doors. Then, as Lucy bent down to get her bag off the floor, we sprinted for The Music Place's toilets instead.

"Do you think she saw us?" Mel panted.

"Hope not," I grinned back, upending my rucksack on to the washbasin counter.

Two hats, two pairs of sunglasses, a black tee, a blue shirt and a blonde wig fell out.

"You can have the wig," Mel said, wriggling into the black T-shirt. She grabbed my hairbrush and pulled it through her crazy curls until she had more or less got her hair flat enough to slip under the black trilby I'd brought.

I yanked on the wig and checked myself out in the mirror. "I've always wanted to be blonde," I said happily. "Em gave me this as a joke for Christmas. I can't believe I'm actually going to wear it!"

"A bit too Summer Collins for my liking," Mel joked. "Here, put this on." She passed me the baseball cap, which I tugged over the wig. Then I buttoned up the blue shirt and and admired the result in the mirror.

"We look totally different," Mel said, twirling beside me. "So long as we don't catch her eye, there's no way Lu'll spot us. This is an excellent idea, Col."

"Cheers," I said modestly, cramming on one pair of sunglasses and handing Mel the other. "Now, let's hang around the CD racks and try not to look obvious, yeah?"

Lucy was still on her own at the table. I checked my watch. Five past. We sidled out of the ladies and up to the Jazz section, discreetly eyeing both the front door and the café every now and again.

"Ten past," Mel said in a low voice over the top of a CD with some dude in sunnies and an old saxophone on the front. "He's not coming."

"Yes he is," I said in excitement. "Look!"

Frankie was jogging down the mall towards The Music Place, checking his watch.

"Wonders will never cease," said Mel, looking

gobsmacked as Frankie pushed open the door of the The Music Place and looked around.

One-nil to Coleen and her faith in humankind! I thought to myself. "I *told* you it would be OK, Mel," I said triumphantly.

Lucy half-rose from her seat and waved to get Frankie's attention. And then it all went wrong.

"SuckER!" Frankie crowed, pointing at Lucy and bursting into raucous laughter. He backed out of The Music Place, ran off down Lions' Walk and disappeared from sight.

The Music Place doors swung shut with the clang of doom. Lucy burst into tears as the other customers gawped. And as me and Mel pulled off our hats and raced over to our mate, I knew I'd just seen the cruellest trick in the world.

Lu didn't comment on the way we'd changed our clothes. She didn't seem to notice my blonde wig either, which tells you what kind of state she was in.

"I...I...I..." she sobbed. "He...he...he..."

"C'mon, Lu," I said as gently as I could. "Let's get out of here."

"Frankie Wilson is a snot-filled, zit-splattered, greasy-haired *flea*," Mel spluttered as we helped Lucy out of The Music Place. "We should *never* have trusted him!"

"Let's go back to mine," I suggested. "Mum'll do us tea and biscuits. A bit of custard cream first aid, yeah?"

"And a nice long list of the ways we're gonna get back at the *flea*," Mel added. "No one treats a mate of ours like that and gets away with it!"

"We'll start by coating his socks in superglue," I said, squeezing Lucy tightly round the shoulders.

"And putting maggots in his lunchbox," Mel snarled.

"And telling everyone at school that he's got nits," I said.

88

Mel stabbed the air with her finger. "And writing in massive chalk letters all over the playground: *Frankie Wilson's breath stinks.*"

Me and Mel went on like this the whole way back to mine. It's amazing how many horrible tricks you can think of when you want to. Lucy just hung her head and let us babble on. She never said a word.

"And finally," I said with a flourish as I pushed open our front door, "we'll put some of Em's special muscle rub in his gym shorts. It burns like crazy. Frankie Wilson'll be hopping all over the place in total agony."

"Right on," Mel agreed.

"Whatever," Lucy said dully.

It was the first thing Lucy had said since leaving The Music Place. OK, so it wasn't much. But it was a start.

"Mum!" I called, dropping my keys on the hall table. "Dad? Em? Anyone here?"

The house was empty. I suddenly remembered: they were all at Em's match.

The kitchen door creaked open, making us all jump.

"Hello Coleen, love," said Nan, smiling at me. "And Mel and Lucy, isn't it?"

Lucy sniffed and wiped her eyes.

Without missing a beat, Nan held open the kitchen door. "There's a nice Battenburg in the cupboard," she said as we trooped in, me and Mel still with our arms wrapped around Lucy. "A bit of cake'll set you right."

"It'll take more than cake, Nan," I sighed as we settled down at the table. And I told her the whole sorry story.

Telling Nan stuff always feels different to telling Mum. Mum's sympathetic most of the time, but I always know she's got half an eye on the stove, or Rascal, or Em's homework, or one of the million other things mums always have to think about. Nan's got the time to really listen, and it's like she's right there in the story with you. She held Lucy's hand the whole way through.

"It sounds like this lad wants a reaction," Nan said when I finished speaking. "Are you going to give him one when you see him on Monday?"

"You bet," I said fiercely.

"He'll get a reaction right where it hurts," Mel agreed.

"So you're going to give him what he wants?" Nan asked.

I frowned. "Is that a trick question?"

"Nothing tricky about it," said Nan, cutting another slice of cake and sliding it on to Lucy's plate. "Just something you might want to think about."

We all munched our cake for a bit.

"Tell me what you thought of Vinny's Vinyl," Nan said into the silence. "Or should I say, The Music Place?"

"It was great," Lucy said quietly. "But I don't want to go back there for a bit."

"I don't suppose you do," Nan said, squeezing her hand.

"I met the old owner," I said, suddenly remembering. "Mr O'Hara, I think he said."

Nan beamed. "Vinny O'Hara? He's still there then?"

"His son runs it now," I said. "And guess what? They've got the original stools in the listening booths again!"

"Those tall white ones?" Nan asked with delight. "Your Pops and I carved our initials underneath one of those stools."

"Nan!" I said, shocked. "You never!"

Nan twinkled at me. "Tucked up high, where no one else could see," she said. "I wonder if they're still there?"

So did I. In fact, at that very instant I decided that I would go back to The Music Place and check out

the stools for myself as soon as I could. I had just had the most brilliant idea for Nan's birthday.

Mel and Lucy stayed till the sky was getting dark, listening to Nan and her stories. I swear, Nan can talk *anyone* out of the dumps. Lucy wasn't exactly dancing on the table when she and Mel headed for home, but she was definitely more cheerful than she'd been all afternoon.

"Thanks, Nan," I said, giving her a hug. Nan's tiny, like me, so we fitted together perfectly.

"Nothing to thank me for, love," said Nan, stroking my hair. "Things'll work themselves out, you know. They always do."

The door jangled. Mum, Dad and Em swept into the hall on a gust of freezing cold air.

"What happened to you today, Coleen?" Mum

asked, hanging up her coat. "That Wilson lad was asking where you were. He seemed ever so upset that you and the others weren't at the match."

What?

"I never want to hear Frankie Wilson's name mentioned in this house again," I snarled, to Mum's astonishment. "Tomorrow, he's *toast*."

Seven

Avenging angels had nothing on me when Monday morning came around.

"And *then* he has the *nerve* to ask my mum why we weren't at the footie!" I stormed at Mel and Lucy on the bus. "I know Nan meant well when she said we shouldn't give Frankie a reaction, but I *can't* not say anything. I just *can't*."

"Me neither," Mel spat.

Lucy was looking practically green with terror at the thought of seeing Frankie in class. "What if he's been telling everyone?" she whispered as the bus whooshed to a halt outside school. "I'll never live it down."

"We'll get to him first," I snarled. "And *he'll* be the one who isn't living."

I was so focused on getting to that classroom in order to give Frankie 'Flea' Wilson a piece of my mind that I barely registered Ben and Jasmine arguing on the school steps.

"But, Jas…"

"You're the most selfish boy I've ever met…"

The words floated into my ears, but then floated out again. You'd think words like that would have me jumping for joy, wouldn't you? But today, I hardly heard them.

But as soon as we crashed through the doors of our form room and glared up and down, it was clear that Frankie wasn't there.

"And you are...?" said the supply teacher sitting in Mr Andrews' chair.

It's quite hard to give your name when your nostrils feel like they're full of steam. The supply teacher looked a bit alarmed as me and Mel snapped out our names and marched over to our places. Lucy trailed behind us, hiding behind her hair the way she always does when she's worried.

"Right," said the supply teacher. "Mr Andrews is sick, so you've got me today. My name is Mrs Holmes, and I'd like a bit of quiet for register."

Mrs Holmes had this really sing-song voice that went up at the end like a ski jump. Listening to her doing register got kind of mesmerising after a bit.

"And last of all," said Mrs Holmes, glancing down the room, "Jimmy Wilson?"

"He's sick too," said Summer. "And he calls himself Frankie, not Jimmy, Miss."

Something whirred deep down in my brain. But before I could work out what the whirring was about, Lucy tugged my sleeve.

"He's not here!" she whispered in relief. "Frankie's not in!"

"That's great, Lu," I said, patting my mate's arm.

To tell the truth, I was feeling like a balloon that was rapidly losing air. I'd been all set to tear a strip off Frankie Wilson, and now I wasn't going to get a chance.

It looked like Mel was feeling the same way. "Drama next," she said as the bell went and everyone packed up their stuff for class. "I hope Miss O'Neill lets me play a really angry person."

"Make that two," I sighed.

Every day that week, I prepared myself to tackle Frankie Wilson. I was determined not to let him off

the hook for what he'd done to Lucy. But every day I was disappointed. Whatever Frankie had, it must have been pretty nasty. I tried to cheer myself up by picturing him vomiting all day and all night. It worked, kind of.

By Thursday, it was clear that Frankie wouldn't be coming into school until the following week.

"Let's forget about him," Mel said as we went into town after school on Friday afternoon. "That little weasel is taking up too much head space."

"You're right," I nodded. "Let's go to Lions' Walk and chill out for a bit."

Lucy looked reluctant at the mention of Lions' Walk.

"Come on, Lu," I coaxed. "It's not Lions' Walk's fault that Frankie Wilson did that to you. Don't let him spoil the stuff you've always enjoyed doing."

With a bit of careful persuasion, we got Lucy as far as the little parade of shops and had a nose around. But when I suggested we got a Coke at The Music Place, she dug her heels in.

"I can't face them in there," she said, shaking her head as we got to the doors.

"They won't even remember," Mel said. "Honest, Lucy. You're worrying about nothing."

The big glass doors of The Music Place swung open with a crash, making us all jump.

"You know where you can stuff that Coke, Ben Hanratty," Jasmine Harris yelled, before running away down the mall with her shiny ponytail flying behind her.

Ben came barrelling out behind her. His trousers were dripping wet and fizzing gently. "I can't stuff it anywhere, can I, Jas?" he shouted back furiously. "You just dumped it all down me!"

"Ben!" Lucy squeaked.

Ben swung round. He looked totally freaked out

when he saw us all standing there and gawping at him.

"Lu!" he mumbled. "I'll… Look… See you later, yeah?" And he took off after Jasmine, leaving a trail of Coke splashes along the way.

"Blimey," I said after a minute, my heart still bouncing around my stomach. Even covered in Coke, Ben Hanratty was gorgeous. "It all kicks off at The Music Place, doesn't it?"

"There you go," Mel said, gently steering Lucy through the swinging doors. "Now they'll be talking about Ben instead of you. You are yesterday's news, babe."

Lucy reluctantly let us guide her into The Music Place café, choosing a corner table where she could sit with her back to everyone else. While Mel ordered us some Cokes, I looked round at the store.

It was nice and busy. There were kids browsing the racks and hanging around the computers. And by the looks of things, three of the six listening booths were in use.

"Three Cokes for you," said Mr O'Hara, bustling up with a tray in his hands.

"Hello, Mr O'Hara," I said, taking our drinks gratefully. "I thought you said you'd retired?"

"I'm working today to help out my son," said Mr O'Hara. "It's good to see the place busy again."

"I'm Coleen by the way," I said.

I introduced Mel and Lucy, and Mr O'Hara shook hands with them both. Watching him bustling back across the café, I suddenly remembered my big plan for Nan's birthday.

"You know what Nan told us about how she'd carved her initials on one of the old stools?" I said to the others in excitement. "What if her and Pops' initials are still there?"

"What are you waiting for?" Mel said. "Go and see!"

102

I pushed back my chair and ran over to the booths. I peeped into the first empty one. Then, hoping no one was about to come in, I bent right down and peered underneath the two white stools. There was a bunch of scribbles, but nothing that looked like initials.

I tried again in the next empty one, and the next one after that. Then I had to wait until the three occupied booths emptied out. I was determined to find Nan's initials. If I could find them, I could put into action the best birthday plan in the world.

Two couples spilt out of two of the booths, smiling goofily at each other and holding hands. I pictured my nan and grandad doing the same thing forty years earlier and sighed, feeling all soppy. Maybe, now Ben wasn't going out with Jasmine any more…

Thinking happily about Ben Hanratty, I looked under the stools again. On the second stool in the second booth, something that looked like **DA + PM** was carved very faintly into the white plastic. I felt a rush of excitement. Nan's name is Doreen, and Pops was called Patrick! But what had Nan's surname been before she married Pops? I realised I didn't know.

"Left something in here, did you?" said Mr O'Hara over the top of the swing door.

I straightened up in a hurry and bumped my head on the stool I'd been staring at. "I was looking for my nan's initials," I explained, feeling a bit stupid as I rubbed my head.

Mr O'Hara rested his hands on the door. "Sounds like you've got a story there," he said.

I told him about Nan's sixtieth birthday, and how Nan and Pops had met over their Beatles track. "So I had this great idea," I explained. "If I could find the right stool, then maybe I could put up a plaque in the booth which had their names on for Nan's birthday. If your son thought it was OK," I added hastily.

"I think it's a wonderful idea," said Mr O'Hara at once. "What a lovely grandaughter you must be, to think of something like that."

"Nan's the lovely one," I said, shuffling my feet and feeling a bit embarrassed.

"You find out if you've got the right initials," said Mr O'Hara, "and I'll suggest it to my son. We could even work out a discount for you if you wanted to have your nan's party here with us, and then reveal your plaque as a surprise at the end. How about that?"

"Perfect!" I said in excitement, picturing a brilliant sixties-themed party at The Music Place. It beat dinner round ours for originality, that was for sure!

"Nan's surname was Adams before she married Pops," I gabbled at Mel and Lucy on Saturday. "I asked Dad last night. So those really are Nan and

Pops' initials from forty years ago on that stool!"

"Brilliant, Coleen," Mel grinned. "So are you going to do this brass plaque then?"

"Mum and Dad think it's a fantastic idea," I said happily. "Dad even told me the date Nan and Pops met in that booth – it sounds like they used to celebrate it like a wedding anniversary in their house. So I'm doing it for *definite*."

"What about the party?" Lucy asked.

"They went for that too," I said, hugging myself with delight. "We're going to have it as a surprise for Nan a week today!"

My head had been spinning ever since Mum and Dad had agreed to my idea. A sixties theme had brought loads of ideas rushing into my brain. Doing my hair in a beehive, maybe. Or making a fabulous sixties minidress out of one of Mum's old flowery pillowcases. Dad would totally have to let me do wild eyeliner, and we'd have the old jukebox in the café playing Beatles tracks all night long. It was shaping up to be a wicked party!

I towed Mel and Lucy into the shoe-repair place on the corner of Lions' Walk where they did little plaques for anything you wanted. I chose the words, and we waited while the engraver wrote it all down exactly as I said it.

"So," I said as we stepped back outside again, "that's the easy part of today over with. Are you ready for the hard part, guys?"

Em's next footie match was against the Western Wanderers in Hartley West, about three miles out of the centre of town. Frankie hadn't missed one of his little brother's football matches yet, and we couldn't believe he would *still* be ill after a whole week. It was time to sort Frankie Wilson out once and for all. So we were all going along for the showdown.

Lucy swallowed. "Ready as I'll ever be," she said.

Arm in arm, we walked down to the market place where the bus stop for Hartley West stood beside the market cross. To my surprise, Ben Hanratty was sitting gloomily on the market-cross steps.

"Hiya," Lucy said, sitting down beside her brother. "Where's Ali and Dave then?"

"Dunno," said Ben with a moody shrug. "They fixed up something without me cos they figured I'd be with Jasmine. But Jas dumped me last night. You probably guessed as much after seeing us at The Music Place."

"That's tough," I said sympathetically. *Yes, yes, yes!* I squealed inside my head.

"You could come to the footie with us if you want," Lucy suggested.

Ben lifted his head. "What footie?" he asked.

I explained about my sister's team, stumbling over my words a bit. It's really weird how Ben scrambles

108

my tongue every time I look at him. "It's only the under-eights, but it's a good laugh," I finished.

"And Frankie's going to be there," Lucy mumbled.

Ben's gaze sharpened. "That moron who stood you up last weekend?"

"That's the one," Mel agreed.

"If that little runt's at the match, I think I'll have a word," Ben said in a dark sort of voice which meant a very nasty word indeed.

"Here's the bus," I said brightly, trying to hide the effect Ben's heroic words had just had on me.

Earth to Jasmine? I thought as we all climbed aboard. *You* dumped *Hartley's answer to Johnny Depp? What were you* thinking *of?*

Eight

"Hiya, Coleen love," Mum called, waving at me. "The match is about to start. There's some tea in the flask if you want it."

"Sorry, Mum," I said, striding past. "Stuff to do. I'll be back in a minute."

Me, Mel, Lucy and Ben walked on up the touchline of the Western Wanderers' pitch to where Frankie Wilson and his dad were standing. I felt like we were in one of those TV shows like *Torchwood*, where the camera goes all slow-mo as

the team stride purposefully towards the lens. A long leather coat would have been good at this point, I decided. But I had to make do with my old puffa instead.

"Frankie Wilson?" Ben growled, coming to a stop inches away from where Frankie was standing. Me, Lucy and Mel clustered around behind Ben, trying to look cool and collected.

"That's me," Frankie said in surprise. "Who are you?"

"Someone you really don't want to meet," said Ben, stepping a bit closer.

"What's going on?" Frankie asked.

"That's what we want to know," said Mel.

"You little worm," I added.

"How could you do something so horrible, Frankie?" Lucy asked, her bottom lip trembling.

Frankie Wilson was looking more and more

bewildered. "What are you on about?" he said.

"Standing Lucy up, you twerp!" I said. "Laughing at her and then running away!"

"But *Lucy's* the one who stood *me* up last weekend," Frankie protested.

Whatever we'd been expecting Frankie to say, we hadn't been expecting *that*.

"*What?*" Mel screeched.

"Are you deliberately messing with our heads?" I demanded.

"Your message!" Frankie turned to Lucy in complete confusion. "The one about meeting in the park instead of The Music Place. I waited for half an hour. Where were you?"

"What message?" Lucy said.

"You know," Frankie insisted. "You gave it to my brother at school, remember?"

"*Brother?*" Mel said in disbelief.

112

A faint memory of Summer Collins' voice earlier that week jogged in my memory.

He calls himself Frankie, not Jimmy, Miss...

Click, clunk, click went the pieces as they all fell into place. A picture suddenly popped into the confusion, as clear as day.

"Your brother," I said weakly. "He's not called – *Jimmy* – by any chance, is he?"

"Back in Cornwall, Jimmy was always the troublemaker at school," Frankie explained, once we were all sitting down and recovering from the shock of discovering that two Frankie Wilsons had been running around Hartley the whole time without anyone noticing. "Being twin brothers meant that I got a lot of stick for the stuff Jimmy was doing. I did my best to get on, but it's pretty tough when people kept expecting me to be as crazy as Jimmy. So when we moved up here, Mum and Dad thought it would be a good idea to put us in different schools."

"Why didn't you say anything about having an identical twin brother?" I asked.

"I probably should have," Frankie admitted. "It would have saved a lot of trouble, I guess. But I liked just being me for a change – not one half of two people. I never thought it would get us into this kind of mess."

"But why does Jimmy call himself Frankie at school?" Mel persisted.

"He never liked his name much," Frankie said with a frown. "Always preferred mine. He probably thought it would be a laugh pretending to be me."

"Maybe he really wants to *be* you," Lucy said.

"Hardly," Frankie snorted. "We don't exactly get on. I should've known Jimmy was up to something when he gave me that message about the park."

I wondered if Lucy had a point. Perhaps Frankie was all the things Jimmy wanted to be. So what better way to be Frankie than to use his brother's name – and then go on and mess up his brother's date?

Ben stuck out his hand. "I owe you an apology, mate," he said.

"Don't worry about it," Frankie replied, shaking Ben's hand.

"Does Jimmy ever come to watch your brother Billy playing?" Lucy asked.

Frankie shook his head. "Jimmy's not into footie the way me and Billy are. He tried to play once, but he had two left feet."

Another reason why Jimmy wants to be Frankie? I wondered. I felt like I was turning into some kind of super-psychiatrist, and it was starting to do my head in.

"So," Frankie said to Lucy. "Now we've sorted

that out, wanna meet up at The Music Place again some time?"

Lucy blushed to the roots of her hair. Looked like lurve was back on the tracks at last.

"How about next weekend?" I suggested, zooming to Lucy's rescue. "Come to my nan's sixtieth birthday party if you like. We're all going to be at The Music Place from about six thirty on Saturday night."

"You'd better have a couple of code words in case Jimmy tries to jinx you guys again," Mel joked.

"How about Doreen and Patrick?" I suggested. "That's my nan and grandad's names."

"Wicked," Frankie said, nodding.

And the shine off Lucy's smile could probably have been seen from outer space.

Back at home, Em was glowing from head to foot

with a top win against the Western Wanderers. Mum pulled a casserole out of the oven that had been cooking for four long lovely hours, and everyone sat down to eat. Well, everyone except Em.

"Three-nil, three-nil," she sang, doing this funny little victory dance around the kitchen. "Three-nil, three-ni-*hil*!"

"Yes, yes," Dad grinned. "Girl of the Match, we know. Well done, love. We're proud as punch."

"Cheers, Dad," Em said, flopping down in her chair at last.

"So you worked everything out with Frankie then?" Mum asked me, ladling out gorgeous steamy bowls of beef casserole and passing them round.

"Totally," I said, attacking my casserole like I hadn't eaten for weeks. "Turns out it's his twin brother Jimmy that's been messing us around at school all along."

"Sounds like this Jimmy needs to be taught a lesson," Dad said.

Ping. My brain lit up. Maybe it *was* time to teach Jimmy Wilson a thing or two about how it felt to be set up. But before I could take that brilliant thought any further, Dad had moved on to the subject of Nan's birthday party.

"We've got both sets of Mum's neighbours lined up," he said, "and your nan's best mate Susan, plus us lot and a couple of mates each for Coleen and Em. Vinny's given us a great deal on a big table in the café. We just need to work out how we're going to get Mum down to The Music Place without letting on."

"Easy," I said promptly. "You guys get set up at The Music Place and me and my mates will drop round to Nan's just as she's getting ready for the birthday tea she still thinks she's getting at our house. I'll tell her I've found her and Pops' initials

118

on that stool, and that she's *got* to come with me to see it before we go back to ours."

"What about the sixties theme?" Em asked. "Can I be Bobby Charlton?"

"You can be whatever you like, love," Dad laughed.

"Bobby Charlton?" I said in disbelief. "He's like, *bald.*"

"Brilliant," Em giggled. "I'll get a special baldie wig, and I've got that old England strip from the sixties that you gave me last birthday, Dad."

I shook my head in despair. My sister is too weird sometimes. Why did she want to be an old footballer when the sixties was famous for some of the best fashion in the world? Are we even *related*?

"We'll get Nan a lovely outfit on Saturday morning," Mum said. "She still loves all the sixties styles, so she'll look perfect for a sixties party; even one that's a surprise."

"What are you going to wear, Coleen?" Dad asked.

"Dad," Em moaned. "Don't be asking her that. We'll all be here for *hours*."

"Zip it, cheeky," I said warningly.

My outfit was going to be a surprise. I needed a can of silver spray paint and some peace and quiet on Saturday afternoon, and ta-da! I was going to knock everyone's socks off.

Thinking these happy thoughts, my brain drifted back to the question of Jimmy Wilson. Now we knew what he was up to, we could turn it in our favour and set *him* up, big time. All my plan needed was a little bit of help from Lucy...

Nine

"So what do you want me to do?" Lucy asked with a frown on the bus on Monday morning.

"Easy," I said. "Play up to Jimmy this week, just like Summer does."

"Ew," Mel said, shuddering.

"Coleen," Lucy began, looking uncertain.

"I don't mean you have to hold his hand or anything," I said hastily. "Just – you know. Laugh at his jokes. Smile at him loads. Make out that you think he's great. Mel and me will help, but you're the key. Jimmy'll lap it up, and then he'll fall into our trap like a prize plum."

The bus pulled into the school bus stop and we all piled off and through the gates.

"OK," said Lucy finally. "I guess he deserves it, right?"

"Good on you," I said, punching Lucy lightly on the arm. "Just think of your yummy date with Frankie on Saturday as your prize."

"With Jimmy Wilson's comeuppance as the cherry on the cake!" Mel giggled.

"Here's your first opportunity, Lucy," said Mel, as Jimmy Wilson came running down the corridor towards us. "Set those teeth to full beam, girl."

Lucy straightened her shoulders. Then she turned her head and gave Jimmy a massive toothy smile as he raced past. Taken totally by surprise, Jimmy cannoned into the lockers that lined the corridors with a massive crash.

"Oh," Lucy gasped. "Are you OK?"

"Sure," said Jimmy, rubbing his knee.

Lucy burst into these massive squeals of laughter. It was so unlike her that I suddenly felt my own mad giggles bubbling up in my tummy. I stared at the walls, frantically looking for something really boring to calm myself down. But when the giggles are about to hit, even posters about fire drills are totally hilarious.

"Ooh, Frankie!" Lucy laughed on and on like a crazy person, helping Jimmy Wilson to his feet. "You're dead funny."

"What did I say?" Jimmy asked in surprise. He glanced at me cautiously. "And what's wrong with your mate?"

My cheeks felt like two fat balloons. I shook my head, determined not to open my mouth and let the giggles out.

"Um..." said Mel, improvising quickly. "Toothache?"

Jimmy looked at Lucy again. She was still grinning at him like a maniac. "Listen," he said at last, "I'm sorry about last weekend. But it was just a laugh, yeah?"

"Don't worry about it," Lucy giggled through gritted teeth. "I've forgotten it already."

"Right," said Jimmy, scratching his head. "Well. See you in class."

"Ow, ow, ow," I moaned as we all ran on up the corridor, leaving Jimmy staring uncertainly after us. "Never try and swallow the giggles, guys. It gives you *massive* indigestion."

It looked like our plan was working. The first person Jimmy smiled at when he came into our classroom was Lucy. Summer looked totally furious, and barged into Lucy's desk when the bell went.

"Whoops," Mel smirked. "Someone's not happy."

"Forget about Summer," I said. "Let's concentrate on getting Jimmy right where we want him. Sitting in the palm of Lucy's hand."

At dinner time, we went and sat on the same table as Jimmy and Ravi. Ravi looked a bit worried. Talking to girls isn't Ravi Singh's strong point.

"Budge up, ladies," said Jimmy cheerfully, "if you want to talk to the King."

"I thought that was Elvis Presley," I said, unable to help myself. Jimmy Wilson was *so* full of himself!

"It usually is," Jimmy said, quick as anything, "but it's his day off today."

We laughed for real at that one. To my surprise, I was warming to Jimmy Wilson. He was really funny when you got past all the boasting and the posing and the naff one-liners. Poor old Ravi just looked gloomily down at the table while Jimmy went on about the weirdest things you can imagine: his brother Billy's rows of old football boots, his mum's obsession with vacuuming their hall carpet, his dad's secret collection of model soldiers.

"And as for my brother Fr— I mean, *Jimmy*," Jimmy went on. "He's so perfect, his teachers give him grades before they even *look* at his homework. He just zones them out with his eyes, and they go: *A, A, A…*" He moved his arms around like an android as he droned the "A, A, A" bit.

"He sounds like a pain," I said, waiting for Jimmy to diss Frankie.

Jimmy shrugged. "Nah," he said. "He's perfect, remember? What's not to like?"

"What did you make of that?" Lucy asked in a low voice as we stacked our dishes and headed out to the playground.

"I think your theory about Jimmy actually wanting

to *be* Frankie is dead on," I said. I was starting to feel guilty about what we were doing here. Then I remembered Jimmy's horrible trick on Lucy, and I hardened my heart. We were going to see this through, for Lucy's sake.

By Friday, I was feeling *seriously* guilty. Whatever Jimmy Wilson had done to Lucy, he *had* apologised. We shared a table with him and Ravi at dinner most days that week (to Summer's disgust), and I swear – I've never laughed so much in my life. And now here we were, sneakily setting him up like a skittle, ready to knock him down.

"Hiya," Jimmy said, looking pleased to see us as we trooped into our classroom on Friday morning. "Listen," he said to Lucy, "do you fancy meeting up this weekend? I mean," he stumbled a bit, "for real this time?"

Me and Mel exchanged glances. This was the moment we'd been building up to all week. Somehow, it felt pretty flat.

"Sure," said Lucy after a minute. "Why don't we try The Music Place again?"

"Really?" Jimmy said in surprise. "You wanna go back there, after – what happened?"

"Like I said, I've forgotten about that," said Lucy. "Six thirty at the café on Saturday sound OK?"

Jimmy beamed. "Great!"

"Why do I feel like a big fat toad?" Lucy whispered to us as we headed on to class.

"We have to sort this once and for all," I said. "And this is the only way to do it."

It was true. But it didn't make me feel any better.

On Saturday morning Mum put her head round my

bedroom door. "Your nan and I are off shopping to get Nan an outfit for tonight," she said. "You coming, love?"

I shook my head. I wasn't really in the mood.

Mum frowned at me. "Are you OK, Coleen? I've never known you to turn down the chance of a shopping trip."

I shrugged. I hadn't slept very well, to tell the truth.

"You're looking peaky," Mum said. "A little trip into town will cheer you up. We can't have you all down in the mouth for Nan's party. We'll get a cake in that coffee place if you like?"

Come on, Col, I said to myself. *Are you really turning down shopping* and *cake, just because you're feeling guilty about Jimmy Wilson?*

"And how about we get you a new necklace or something?" Mum suggested.

That clinched it.

"Well," I said slowly, "I do need something space-agey for my outfit tonight."

We took Nan to the big department store in town. There are loads of little boutiques full of the stuff she likes in there. I spotted something almost as soon as we went inside.

"There," I said, pouncing on a lemon-coloured dress with a fitted bodice and a swirly skirt. "What do you think?"

Nan loved it. By the time we'd bought that, and a pair of cute yellow shoes to go with it, and a massive slice of chocolate cake at my favourite café, and a brilliant chunky chrome-chain necklace for me, I was fizzing with excitement about the party and hardly worrying about Jimmy Wilson at all.

"We'll see you round at ours about seven then,

Doreen?" Mum said as we left Nan's house with a wave.

"See you then, love," Nan called.

Giggling quietly together, me and Mum linked arms and strolled back round to ours.

After a quick bite of lunch, I took myself off down the bottom of the garden to sort out my outfit. Dad has an old shed down there where he keeps his tools, old tins of paint and cans of smelly stuff like white spirit and engine oil. Dad had been a bit surprised when I'd asked if I could use the can of silver car paint he had sitting on a shelf in there.

"Make sure you spray it out in the garden," Dad had warned. "That stuff stinks and will riddle your brain with holes if you do it inside."

I carefully put down four big black binbags on the patio and placed the minidress that I'd made out of an old pillowcase on the top. Fixing on a mask the way Dad had shown me, I started blasting the pillowcase with the spray paint. When one side of the dress was dry, I turned it over and did the other. I was going to wear my knee-high black boots and my new chain necklace with it, plus my blonde wig and a little black peaked cap of Mum's.

"Twiggy, eat your heart out," I murmured, twirling about in front of the long mirror in our hall when I'd finished.

Mum and Dad were dashing around upstairs, getting their outfits sorted. It was gone five o'clock, and they were all supposed to have gone over to The Music Place by now to help get everything ready. I was going to stay and wait for Mel and Lucy, and then we were going round to fetch Nan at five thirty.

"Great outfit, Col," Em said, clattering downstairs in her Bobby Charlton kit. "Very Bond girl."

"Cheers," I said. I glanced at Em's baldie wig. "You

132

look, er," I said, fishing around desperately for something nice to say, "very… footballey."

"I know," Em said happily. "Great, isn't it?"

"Make sure you get Nan to The Music Place for six thirty, Coleen," Mum fretted, layering on some extra eyeliner at the hall mirror while Dad slicked back his hair with some stinky grease in the mirror behind her. "Think you'll be OK?"

"Sorted," I said. "Go on – you'll be late!"

"Do you think we've really got time for this, Coleen?" Nan asked as me, Mel and Lucy hurried her down Lions' Walk. "We can't be late for your mum and dad. It's almost six thirty!"

Nan looked brilliant. The lemon-coloured dress swirled around her like a cloud, and her yellow shoes made a lovely clickety-clack noise on the pavement.

"You have to see this," I said, steering her down towards The Music Place. "Your initials are as clear as anything. We've got loads of time to get back home."

"If you say so," Nan said doubtfully.

I glanced at Mel and Lucy and winked. They both looked excellent. Mel was wearing a pair of gold trousers and a brown top, with these huge gold earrings swinging from her ears and her hair all fluffed up into the biggest Afro I'd ever seen. Lucy's new blue jacket looked adorable over a cute little miniskirt, and her mum had helped to style her hair up into this fantastic beehive.

We could hear *Twist and Shout* pumping out of the Wurlitzer as we pushed open the glass doors of The Music Place.

"SURPRISE!" shouted everyone.

Nan goggled at the table all laid up with fantastic food, at Mum and Dad dancing around the jukebox,

and at Em grinning madly from underneath her horrible baldie wig.

"Is this all for me?" she gasped.

"Of course it is, Nan," I laughed, and gave her a smacking kiss. "Happy birthday!"

Nan wandered up the steps to the café in a daze as her guests cheered and clapped. Me and my mates exchanged high fives. We'd done it!

A blond lad in a nice checked shirt came down the steps towards us.

"Hi," he said with a grin. "Great party!"

I started to smile back. But then I panicked. Was this Frankie – or Jimmy?

Ten

Panic was all over Lucy and Mel's faces too. It was clear that they were wondering the same thing. How could we find out which twin we were looking at without giving away our plan?

"Hi," I said, a little wildly. "Great to see you, er…"

"Frankie," said Frankie/Jimmy, looking a little confused.

Of course, that didn't help. We knew Frankie as Frankie, *and* Jimmy as Frankie!

"You remember this is for my nan's birthday?" I

gabbled on. "Doreen?" I waggled my eyebrows at Frankie/Jimmy and hoped in desperation that I had the right Wilson twin.

"Oh yeah," said the lad, his brow clearing. "And your grandad was Patrick, right?"

"Frankie," I said in relief, "it *is* you."

"I *said* it was," Frankie said, rolling his eyes. "What, are you expecting Jimmy too?"

On cue, the big glass doors swung open behind us all. Jimmy stepped into The Music Place.

"The King is here!" he said, grinning and spreading his arms out wide.

And then the grin fell off his face as he saw us standing beside his brother.

The likeness was incredible. Down to the last freckle, Frankie and Jimmy Wilson were like mirror images. Talk about weird, seeing them both standing there like that, gawping at each other.

137

"Frankie Wilson?" said Mel. "Meet Frankie Wilson."

"Did anyone ever tell you how much you guys look alike?" I added.

Jimmy just stood there, rooted to the spot like someone had glued the soles of his shoes to the floor. It was awful, but kind of funny at the same time.

"Hi, Jimmy," Frankie said, sounding quite cool. "Back on the scene of the crime?"

"It was just a laugh, that stunt last weekend," Jimmy said nervously. "Sorry, mate. Anyway," he said, turning to Lucy, "I thought we'd sorted all that out?"

"We did," Lucy said. "But we didn't get the whole truth of it, did we, Jimmy?"

"I know," Jimmy said. He shuffled his feet a bit. "Not the kind of thing that perfect Frankie would do. And here I am, plain old Jimmy Wilson, and I can see you lot all standing there hating my guts."

"We did," I said. "But we don't any more."

Jimmy looked hopeful. "Really?" he said.

"Really," I replied.

"So," Jimmy said cautiously, "are you gonna be mates with both Frankie *and* Jimmy Wilson then?"

"Looks that way," said Mel.

"Blimey," said Jimmy. "I don't think that's ever happened, has it, Frankie?"

"Nope," Frankie grinned.

"There's a first time for everything," I said, grabbing both Wilson twins and pushing them up the steps towards the party food.

It was nearly time for my big birthday surprise. All the food had been cleared off the plates and the bottles of wine and juice were practically empty. Dad was groaning quietly at one end of the table, complaining that he'd eaten too many pickles in his burger, and Em's baldie wig hung on the back of her chair ("It's so hot!" she'd complained to me, pulling it off somewhere halfway through the meal). Frankie and Lucy were nose to nose at the window, talking about some new band they'd heard recently. Me and Mel had spent most of the meal cheering Jimmy up. It turned out he'd really liked Lucy after all.

"I should've had that date with Lucy when I got the chance, instead of behaving like a prize idiot," he sighed over his Coke.

"Plonker," I said. "Anyway, there's always Summer. She'd go out with you again in a flash."

"I can't blame her," Jimmy smirked, perking up at once. "I am a total love god after all."

Mum stood up just as me and Mel fell about laughing.

"Doreen?" she said. "We've got a special surprise for you."

"Another one?" Nan asked. "I don't think I can take much more!"

Mum winked at me. "Over to you, Coleen!"

"Remember how I told you about the initials on the stool, Nan?" I said, helping my nan out of her chair.

"No need to apologise, love," Nan said, flapping her hands at me. "I should've known too much time had passed for you to have found our initials after all these years. And I've had such a lovely time tonight."

"Well, I found them," I said, smiling. "They were in this booth, right over here."

I guided her down the café steps. Everyone else followed close behind. Mr O'Hara stood behind the counter, polishing glasses and grinning at me as I pushed open the door to the second booth along. The plaque twinkled on the wall, set neatly just above the CD player.

Doreen and Patrick

24 September 1967

All You Need Is Love

Best Mates Mirror

Give your bedroom a friendly facelift by decorating your mirror with photos of your best friends. Now you'll be reminded of them every morning!

ASK AN ADULT BEFORE YOU GET CUTTING!

HAVE FUN!

You will need:

 A mirror (large or small it doesn't matter)

 Photos of your friends

 Pretty wrapping paper (sparkly paper is my fave)

 Plain card

 Double-sided sticky tape

 PVA glue or Pritt Stick

 Scissors

PLEASE TAKE CARE WITH BOTH
THE MIRROR AND THE SCISSORS!

Step 1

Draw shapes on to the plain card –
hearts, stars, flowers, triangles – and cut
them out. Trace around the card shapes
on to the wrapping paper and cut out
the paper shapes.

Step 2

Glue the paper shapes
to the matching card
shapes, so the shapes
are rigid.

Step 3

Trim the photos of
your friends into
cute heart shapes.

Step 4

Attach double-sided
tape to the back of
the photos and shapes
and stick them on to
the frame of your mirror.

Step 5

To add some glitz, use the
back of your ruler to curl
gift-wrap ribbon
into cute little
twists and stick
those on too.

VOILÀ!

YOUR GORGEOUS BEST MATE MIRROR!

You could also try...

★ Adding photos of your pets.

★ Printing cute pictures and designs
off the Internet to add too.

★ Bling it up by adding some glittery
rhinestones or sequins.

COMING SOON!

Coleen
Style Queen

Rock That Frock!

Are you lacking the X-factor? Need some extra
sparkle on stage? Then maybe I can help. I'm
Coleen and I love fashion, friends and having fun.

Me and my mates are entering the local
singing competition this summer. Lucy's got
the voice, Mel's got the moves and I've
planned some rockin' outfits!

Turn the page for a sneak preview...

HarperCollins *Children's Books*

OK, so a bit of advice here. Never go dancing in a strapless top. Especially if you're at the gig of your absolute favourite band. Bubby, that is, whose songs make you want to go mental on the dancefloor.

"You OK, Coleen?" my mate Mel yelled over the thumping music. She looked fab in a Bubbly T-shirt and a new pair of skinny jeans, with her huge cloud of hair catching the lights.

"I'm great!" I yelled back, dancing like crazy while hanging on to my top with both hands. I had a feeling I looked a bit weird.

All the old beardy-bloke portraits started wobbling on the Town Hall walls as Bubbly – the best band *ever* – revved up for the chorus of their massive hit, *Wave Like You Mean It.* The kids packing out the Town Hall floor started going even crazier, waving their arms madly in the air. I clutched my top with one hand and waved desperately with the other, wishing for the millionth time that I'd worn something a teensy bit more sensible.

"Get your arms up, Coleen!" my other mate Lucy laughed, her long hair flying all around her like a blonde halo. As usual, she was plainly dressed in a neat little blouse and ironed jeans. "C'mon, go for it!"

"*Wave, wave, wave like you mean it,*" sang the band, along with the whole of the audience. "*If there's a better way, I ain't seen it; wave, wave, wave like you mean it, whoo!*"

The lead singer of Bubbly is called Deena. She looked totally wicked in her hot pink skinny jeans, and I completely adored the cropped cardie she was wearing over a black string-vest top. Her hair was streaked all these different colours, and she was jumping around in high-heeled gold shoes like she was wearing trainers. You've got to admire that. The two guitar players, Lori and Jammie, were doing these leaps from side to side like a pair of funky kangaroos – Lori flicking her long, jet-black hair from side to side and Jammie's bleach-blond quiff gelled straight up into the air.

"*If there's a better way, better way, we ain't seen it, whoo!*" Deena sang, pumping the air with her hands.

The song thundered on through Lori's final guitar solo and a *crash-crash-crash* from the drummer, Belle, with her snaky blonde plaits. This really was my last chance. Heaving my top up, I clenched the middle bit between my teeth and threw both my hands into the air, just as...

"Thank you!" Deena yelled as the song died away and the audience went bananas.

Typical.

"Hartley," Deena went on, "you're the best home town ever!"

I forgot about my top troubles at that, and screamed "Yay!" along with the rest of the hall. The whole of Hartley was dead proud of Bubbly. They had even gone to school at Hartley High – though that had been a bit before my time.

After two more encores, we all streamed out of the Town Hall, blinking a bit in the low-lying sunshine of the late afternoon. The music had been so loud that my ears were still ringing – plus my head was full of how I was going to recreate Bubbly's look as *soon* as I got home. They were so cool, they were practically frozen!

"Wow!" Lucy giggled, pushing back her hair. "That rocked!"

"Wicked!" Mel agreed as she wiped her forehead.

"What?" I said to Mel, sticking a finger in one of my ringing ears.

"WICKED!" Mel roared at me.

"Trust Mel 'the Mouth' Palmer to be showing off on the Town Hall steps," said a snidey voice behind us.

We turned round to see Summer Collins, Hartley High's worst specimen, who also happened to be in my class, coming out of the gig. Her two best mates, Hannah Davies and Shona Mackinnon were standing next to her. To say that Summer and her mates aren't my favourite people in the world would be like saying chocolate-flavoured lip gloss is OK: in other words, a massive understatement! Unfortunately they are all in our class so we have to live with them – like you have to live with a crop of spots when they pop up on the end of your nose.

Today, Summer and her mates were all wearing exactly the same pink hoodies and sparkle-encrusted trainers. They are so *sad*!

"Uh-oh," I said, not missing a beat. "It's the Three Clones." I whipped my head around, pretending to look scared. "How many more of you are there? Are you taking over the world?"

Summer tossed her hair. "Come on, you two," she said to Hannah and Shona. "We've got better things to do on a Saturday afternoon than talk to a bunch of losers."

"So have we!" Mel called cheerily after Summer as she stalked away with her friends in tow. "Like finding the scientist who cloned you all and asking him really nicely to stop before he makes any more!"

"Anyone fancy going for a drink somewhere?" Lucy said when I'd finally stopped laughing. Mel just cracks me up!

"Can't," I said, catching my breath. "Stuff to do."

"Don't tell me you're going to do your homework," said Mel in horror.

"There's tomorrow night for that," I said, waving my hand to kill the homework ghost before it ruined my weekend. "No," I continued, "I have *fashion plans.*"

I'm famous for my fashion plans. It doesn't take much to inspire me, and then I'm away on my Next Big Thing.

"Ooh," said Lucy. "What are you planning?"

"Think Rock Chick," I said, tapping my nose. "It's my new inspiration. When you see me tomorrow, you won't recognise me!"

To be continued...

Design a T-shirt and win a
PINK NINTENDO DS
and a fashion designer game!

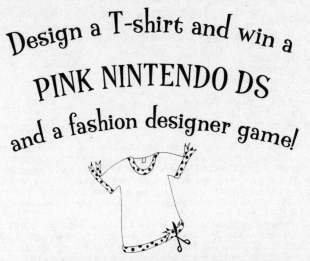

Are you a Style Queen like Coleen? Would you
love to see your own designs brought to life?

Now's your chance to get creative by entering this
fab competition to design your own T-shirt. Simply
draw your design on a piece of paper and send it,
along with your name, address and email, to:

Coleen Style Queen T-shirt comp
HarperCollins Children's Books Marketing
77-85 Fulham Palace Road
London W6 8JB

The winner – to be chosen by Coleen McLoughlin –
will win a pink Nintendo DS with
"Fashion Designer: Style Icon" game, plus one
T-shirt made up to their own design.

Closing date for entries – 30th September 2008.

Get designing!